a min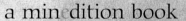dition book
*published by Penguin Young Readers Group*

*Copyright © 2005 by Werner Thuswaldner*
*Illustrations copyright © 2005 by Robert Ingpen*
*Rights arranged with "minedition" Rights and Licensing AG, Zurich, Switzerland.*
*Coproduction with Michael Neugebauer Publishing Ltd. Hong Kong.*

*Manufactured in Hong Kong by Wide World Ltd.*
*Typesetting in Carmina, designed by Gudrun Zapf-Hesse.*
*Color separation by Fotoreproduzioni Grafiche, Verona, Italy.*

*Library of Congress Cataloging-in-Publication Data available upon request.*

*ISBN 0-698-40032-1*
*10 9 8 7 6 5 4 3 2 1*
*First Impression*

*For more information please visit our website: www.minedition.com*

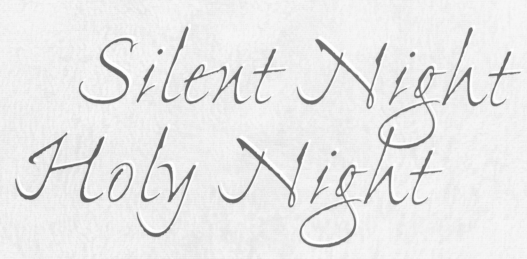

# Silent Night
# Holy Night

## a Song for the World

Werner Thuswaldner

and Patricia Crampton

Pictures by Robert Ingpen

minedition

"Silent night, holy night": the hymn whose serenity restores us — men, women and children — to the peace which is our true home.

Millions of people know the melody, some know the verses, but very few are aware of more than a grace and blessed consolation of beyond the carol. Very few know anything of its mysterious birth, the seed of its magic, and the source of its power.

At Christmastime, early in the nineteenth century, two friends, one a curate, Joseph Mohr, the other a teacher and organist, Franz Xaver Gruber, were living in the Austrian village of Oberndorf on the river Salzach. War had been raging in the area, the bridge collapsed, cannonballs wrecked the houses, stifling smoke filled the streets. Many had died when foreign soldiers invaded and looted the village.

In the winter it seemed as if the cold would never end. When the river froze, there was hardly any work, as most of the men were bargees, transporting salt by barge from the mountains to the great cities. Salt was so precious in those days that it was known as "white gold." In the grip of a long winter, the spark of hope almost died among the people.

Even when the ice melted, the Salzach, set free, came leaping down from its mountain gorges, tossing aside the houses on its banks. Time and again, a bargee and his family, home and living gone, would face ruin. These people were no strangers to hunger and want, grief and suffering.

The young priest, Joseph Mohr, and the organist Franz Xaver Gruber were equally familiar with poverty: both came from poor families. Mohr, from the city of Salzburg, had never known his father, who was said to have been a musketeer. His mother earned the family's meager living by knitting garments. His godfather had actually been the town's executioner.

Thanks to the observant priest, Joseph was helped to develop his gifts and attended school and university, training to become a curate, directed from one parish to another across the country. Oberndorf was his second appointment.

A cheerful soul, Joseph smoked a long pipe,
sat in the inn with the bargees, drank with them
and accompanied their songs on the guitar.

Franz Xaver Gruber had been lucky, too. Left to his parents, he would have had to stay at home and work at the weaver's loom beside his brothers and sisters. But he, too, worked hard at school and especially enjoyed his music lessons. His father reluctantly agreed to let Franz become a teacher, but loving music as he did, he spent every spare moment at the organ, playing, and composing tunes of his own. Music comforted him through many family tragedies: of his twelve children only four survived (even though he would end up outliving his friend Joseph by fifteen years).

The two men decided to give the sorely tried villagers of Oberndorf a Christmas present: a song, to rouse them from the misery of despair.
Mohr offered his friend a poem he had written, and within a short time, Gruber had set it to music. The church organ was in a sorry state, so they decided to perform the new song at the end of the midnight Mass, with a guitar accompaniment.

Rumors of a special event had
spread through the village ahead
of the mass, and excitement rose
when the two men walked in and
began to sing.

Mohr played the guitar, and the
congregation in the candlelit
church began to join in the
refrain, as if they had always
known this newly-created hymn.

Borne up by the miracle that had come on them on that silent, holy night, they walked home through the snow with lighter hearts, the first to hear the carol whose heavenly message now encompasses the world.

Only light, the radiant light of a visionary inspiration, could travel so swiftly, from a little Austrian village to the most distant corners of the world. Missionaries helped to carry its joyful news into places and times undreamed-of by Joseph and Franz Xaver.

Even this: one Christmas season during World War I, in the most dreadful days of all, between a thousand and a thousand deaths, men walked toward each other. Enemies, wondering, sharing "the air of an old Austrian song," and coming closer, saw, not enemies, but themselves, in that redeeming dawn.

Now, when people hear the carol, they feel just as the worshippers felt at that midnight Mass in Oberndorf. No one could claim it for the glitzy world of the supermarkets, on the city's commercial streets. It does not promise children loads of presents for Christmas. Instead, it stirs the hearts of everyone, as they sense the beauty of modesty and humility, and remember when they, too, were little children.

Silent night, holy night,
All is calm, all is bright,
Round yon virgin, mother and child,
Holy infant, so tender and mild:
Sleep in heavenly peace,
Sleep in heavenly peace.

Silent night, holy night,
Sheperds quake at the sight.
Glories stream from Heaven afar,
Heavenly hosts sing alleluija;
Christ, the Saviour is born,
Christ, the Saviour is born.

Silent night, holy night,
Son of God, love's pure light,
Radiant beams from thy holy face,
With the dawn of redeeming grace:
Jesus, Lord, at thy birth,
Jesus, Lord, at thy birth.

Whenever the song is heard, it recreates the atmosphere of that far-off Christmas night, when Joseph and Franz Xaver began to sing the simple melody in Oberndorf church; when the listeners, as they joined in the refrains, forgot all the want and misfortune they had known, and turned their thoughts to the holiest night of all.